Death Was
Natural __
Murder __
Accident __
Suicide __
(other) __

To instigate an investigation, it must first be determined if there is reason for investigation.

It is sometimes not easy to make a determination.

Er, in what way is there "other"?

Contents

About the author

CD Moulton has traveled extensively over much of the world both in the music business, where he was a rock guitarist, songwriter and arranger and in an import/export business. He has been everything from a bar owner to auto salvage (junkyard) manager, longshoreman to high steel worker, orchid grower to landscaper, tropical fish farmer to commercial fisherman. He started writing books in 1983 and has published more than 350 books as of January 1, 2023. His most popular books to date are about research with orchids, though much of his science fiction and fantasy work has proven popular. He wrote the CD Grimes, PI series, and the Det. Nick Storie series, Clint Faraday series, and many other works.

He now resides in Gualaca, Chiriqui, Panamá, where he writes books, plays music with friends, does research with orchids and medicinal plants. He has lately become involved in fighting for the rights of the indigenous people, who are among his closest friends, and in fighting the extreme corruption in the courts and police in Panamá.

He offers the free e-book, *Fading Paradise*, that explains what he has been through because of the corruption.

CD is the discoverer of the Chadam Protocol for curing cancer.

Facebook page Ambrosia peruviana for cancer.

"What we have here is a question of what I am to put on the death certificate," Doctor Elias Quintero, ME, such as they had for the town of Cusapin, Comarca Ngobe Bugle, Bocas del Toro, Panama, said to the assembled police [also such as they had on the comarca] and medical personnel, natural medicine woman, court officer [such as they had on the comarca],and a couple of random curiosity seekers.

"I don't get it!" Raul Dormiendo, a curious bystander, cried. "He's dead! Isn't that all that has to be on some stupid paper for the Panamanian government to try to find something wrong with the date or something?"

The comarca held such meetings informally, at this stage. They were as close to "official" as things were on the comarca.

"This would be called an inquest in the city," Nito Faraday A. replied. "It's, like you say, for a paper that we have to file with the government. Gordon Roberts wasn't a Panamanian, much less a Ngobe. He probably has some kind of insurance, and that kind of thing. They want to know if they have to pay. That kind of thing."

Nito was as close to a head of violent crimes as they had on the comarca.

"Well, what kind of thing do you have to say?" Yajira Silvio, medicine woman, asked.

"I have to check a box on the certificate," Enrique Smith, judge, such as they had on the comarca, explained. "It is for natural death, murder, accidental death, suicide, or other."

"Other? What other is there?" Naldo Smith asked.

"Hmm. Nito?" Enrique asked.

"In this case, voodoo, or spirit caused."

"We can say any of the others if it was the spirits. Maybe not, if it was voodoo," Yajira said. "How will we find out?"

"We have people here who knew the man," Nito suggested. "We will have them tell what they know. Maybe the answer will come up.

"The background will be that he has been here for about six months. He came from Baton Rouge, Louisiana, in the estados. He was a truck driver with his own company that he sold when he moved to Panama. He had no real criminal record. Just a few petty things, such as a couple of fights they called assault,there.

He gambled, but not much. He drank, but not too much. He smoked pot, sometimes. He had a wife of twelve years, a son ten years old, and a daughter four years old. He left them, but it was arranged that they would be taken care of before he left. There weren't strong feelings expressed in the divorce case, only that they didn't want to live together anymore and mutually agreed to divorce. He associated with some shady characters, but that was a given in the long-haul trucking business. His health was very good for a 54 year old man. He was neither fat nor slim. What we call a bullish build. His personality was variable. He was a bigot against blacks, but not against us Indios, and a little against the Chinese, but not against the Japanese. He was not religious, that we know, though he marked "Catholic" on a few papers. He did not attend church services. He was heard to remark that he was a Catholic, but not a good one, in a bar in Bocas. He was considered cheap, by some. He was not a Boquete Gringo, but wasn't far from it, sometimes.

"A few other things, but we can't know if they are important. Yet.

"Samuel, he rented that house from you, and you were with him more than anyone else, here. Tell us about him, as you knew him.

"Any secrets may be critical, and he's dead, so they can't hurt him, now. Do not break any promises you made, if he was honorable."

Samuel Doros sighed and grimaced. "Well, we shared a few secrets, but not with any promises.

He was part honorable, and part ... not so much.

"I remember when he came. He was at Gloria's cantina....

"He came in his fancy boat, and I was there for almuerza. He spoke a little Spanish, but more like Mexican, but different. Kind of like Mexican and Cuban, mixed, with a little Colombian thrown in. Some that I suppose was French.

"Anyhow ....."

"Hi! Call me Gordy. I'm from Louisiana, in the states, you know.

"Do you speak English? Most people here don't get my Spanish."

"I speak some English. I am Samuel Doros. I live here, most of the time, but I go to Bocas Isla, sometimes, and to David."

"Great! I like this place! It's what you call tranquilo, and you people are great! No big phony front and brag about what you got when you ain't got nothing to brag about, anyhow."

Samuel laughed. "I speak English. Not that!"

"You people are great! Say what you mean, and ain ... aren't mean about it. You laugh, so I know it's just fun.

"I know my English is rotten. Don't worry if you tell me I don't make no sense. I know it!

"Would it be alright if I stay here? I mean, they told me I had to get what they call "approved" before I can stay more than one night.

"Is there anyplace for rent? I couldn't afford a hotel ... but that's even cheaper than rent in a flophouse in the states."

"If I understand, you can stay so long as you don't make an obnoxious ass out of yourself like some gringos do.

"I have a little house my son uses when he's here, but he doesn't come much. I suppose you could rent it. I can use the money anytime I go to David."

"How much? By the month?"

"Whatever you think is fair."

"Really? What if I think five bucks a month is fair?" Gordy laughed.

Samuel shrugged. "If you *honestly* think that is fair."

"I'll be damned! You make a guy feel like a doofus for even thinking something.

"How about two hundred a month?"

"That is too much. It is small, and doesn't have a refrigerator or washer or hot water – not that anyone else does. No electricity, a lot of the time.

"How about seventy five a month? That's all I spend if I go to David."

"You aren't even real! I love you! I love your people! Sold!"

Samuel showed him the house, which was the same as the others close. It was crude, but clean and comfortable. Gordy was pleased, and made arrangements for his boat to be docked and his few belongings to be stored, what he didn't take to the house. His neighbors were curious and friendly. He seemed suspicious, at first, then fit well into the culture, then slowly became a bit suspicious again. Samuels asked him what was wrong.

"I'm a bigot, some things. There were two black dudes at the cantina and hotel who made total asses of themselves. They don't fit here, but the people just laughed and avoided them.

"I don't know what they wanted here. They don't fit."

"Oh, yes. The two drug runners. They come by every couple of months. They are not allowed to stay, but they wouldn't, anyway. No one likes them."

"You know they're drug dealers and you don't stop them?"

"Why would we? We don't use their drugs, and we don't let them use them here, and we would chop them up if they tried to make anyone here use them. Why would we try to stop them from going to places that have made them even possible?

"They fit with their type. They don't fit here.

They have no place here, and almost no place there. Their lives are empty. It is their own doing. Leave us alone, and we'll leave you alone.

"You see, all of 'us' alone against one of 'you' alone. It is sad, but it is what it is. They can be alone in a group. We aren't. A life alone, in its many senses, is not worth the energy."

"God! I love you people!"

"Samuel, I think I'm falling in love with Gisela."

"Why tell me? Tell her."

"But ... I'm a gringo!"

"And?"

"Would it, I mean, be alright? A Gringo and a woman of the people?"

"You know the Smiths, and the Trotmans, and the Faradays. Why would you think they have such names if we did not approve?"

"God! I love you people!"

"Gordy! There were two men from Louisiana here. They asked about you."

"Oh, God! No! Who ... I mean, what did they want?"

"They did not seem to be honest people. Jira said they are not. We told them nothing. They said they were business partners back north, but they did not seem to be of a type of partners you would have. They were uncivilized, and made threats. They were told to be off the comarca by nightfall.

"The one they called Freddie and the one they called Ahmad. Freddie was white, but Ahmad was black. They are very crude people."

"Samuel, I have tried to be honest with you, but there are things I didn't tell you. I was afraid you'd make me leave.

"I was in the business of ... I was *used* in the business of distributing drugs. They used my trucks. They threatened my family. I came here to get away from that.

"Sam, my wife's name was Glenda Feratti. She was from a mafia family. I didn't know that when I married her, but that was more because I didn't want to know. I didn't want to believe all the stories about her parents.

"She's still running the business. She's afraid I'll rat on them.

"Sam, I wouldn't. I just want away from it, and never to see any of them again. Even the woman I once loved.

"She turned my own children against me. I don't care if I never see them again, either.

"That's a lie. I want to save them from her.

"Sam, I just want them to leave me alone! They say that, once I'm in, I can never get out again. I came here to get out, and it was working.

"What can I do? I do *not* want any of them to ever come here!"

"We will see that they don't come here. You have been a friend, and we will help you in any way we can. We will declare them outlaw if they ever return. They made threats of physical assault against the people. That is intolerable, and we will not tolerate it.

"I will see that anyone who asks about you in any way is told nothing."

"Maybe they're just trying to find out where I am, but ... why would they come here? How did they know ... maybe someone saw me and told them."

"When Max told them he didn't know where you were, they said they found your boat, registered in your name, so they knew you were here, and they had ways to make him tell them.

"Amos was there, and he said they would have to face the whole village for such threats, and would end up chopped to ragged pieces with dull machetes if they ever did anything like that again. It is why they were ordered to leave."

"I see. Freddie and Ahmad are what're called enforcers. They're very dangerous people. I don't want anyone here involved. They could be hurt, or even killed."

"Or *they* could be hurt or killed. We will not abandon a friend."

"Sam, I'm going to do something so you can say I left, and be telling the truth. It is a way they use to say a truth that somebody will think is true, but it is a lie if you say it a different way. It's called a used car argument. Tell a partial truth, but stop there, and don't tell more."

"Like, I stopped drinking, but don't say you started again next night?"

Gordy laughed a dry laugh. "Like I stopped drinking Saturday and don't say I started drinking again Sunday.

"They might not come back. In fact, *they* won't, but there may be others that do come."

"So we will tell anyone who asks the partial truth."

Gordy hugged him.

"This is Gladys Donell," Chapo introduced to Sam. "She is a friend of that gringo who was at your place last week, or whenever."

This is what was arranged.

"Gordon? You know him from Louisiana?" Sam asked.

"Well, I'm a very good friend of his wife. Ex-wife. I want to tell him she wants him to come home. Just for awhile. For the kids, you know."

"Well. I am not too familiar with any of his family. He left two days ago. He said he was going in the direction of Medellin or Cartagena.

He knew some people there, once."

"Oh? I didn't think he would go anywhere near Colon ... how strange!"

"To tell the truth, he didn't like his ex-wife, and wouldn't go back, anyhow. He wants to be in a place she wouldn't even look."

"He's smarter than we thought." She said it, in a very hard voice.

A tall black man came to stand beside her and asked if she'd learned anything. She introduced him as Liam LeFleur, from New Orleans. Perhaps they had heard of him.

"Why would we know about anyone from New Orleans, or anywhere else in France?"

The look on her face was priceless! She looked like she had been slapped with a wet fish.

"Er, that is, uh, she means New Orleans, Louisiana," Liam said. "In the United States. You are correct in asking why you would hear of me in Panama.

"I am a priest, but not of the Catholic church.

"I passed a woman near the dock who has some power, so you will know what kind of priest."

"A woman? With power?" Chapo asked. "What do you mean? Power?"

"Power of the psyche," Gladys said. "Liam is a voodoo priest. He says Gordon is here. His power told him. He can trace an amulet Gordon carries."

"Perhaps he can find an amulet, but not necessarily the person who once carried it?" Sam asked. That got him a hard look. Yajira had found the medallion almost immediately. She could sense that kind of thing. The medallion was in the shed by the dock where Gordy stored his boat before he re-registered it as a homemade fishing boat, property of Amos Jaramillo of El Flor, Chiriqui.

Liam said he went directly to it when they docked, an hour before. It proved that Gordon had been there!

"No one ever said he wasn't, only the fact that he had left two days before in the direction of Colombia," – and that no more information would be given to a person who acted in such an arrogant manner, and that it was suggested, very pointedly, that Liam and his lady friend be off the comarca by nightfall, and not return. There was no reason they could give why the people on the comarca would care whether some gringo located some other gringo or not – was there?

"You'd better be careful! I have powers!" Liam snarled.

Yajira, who just joined them, at that point, said, "You have the ability to locate certain patterned crystal structures. It is no more. You can sense I have a talent, also. Perhaps *I* who should be threatening *you*! My powers might well far exceed yours."

"Whatever, you are not welcome here," Sam replied, calmly. "Go! Vete! Begone!"

"Let's not get off on the wrong foot, here!" Gladys cried. "We just want to try to get him to go home to his family! His children need their father!"

"You cannot lie to me. You are evil," Yajira said. "You bring a voodoo priest on your journey of good will and concern?

"Whatever," Sam said. "You have been told to leave. Leave. Do not return." He and Yajira turned and walked away. Chapo shook his head, shrugged, and left.

Liam and Gladys stood there a minute, then headed toward the town. They went to the cantina, where Nito was talking with friends over coffee. When they came in, he said, "It's getting a bit late. You had better leave now, or you won't make Chiriqui Grande by dark."

They headed toward the dock.

As they were heading out in their speedboat, Gordy came to say, "I think they will be back. Some of them. It will cause a lot of problems for you. I can't live with that. I'll go."

"They won't cause anything more than a momentary inconvenience," Nito said. "We'll handle them."

"You can't know the kind of monsters they are!" Gordy protested. "I know. They'll never stop. You don't know what they are!"

"You ever hear of Clint Faraday?" Yajira asked.

"Clint Faraday? I've heard ... wasn't he a detective that caught umpty dozen killers and international hoods?"

"Yeah. He was Nito's father. I think Nito knows a lot about the type."

Gordy looked thoughtful, nodded, looked a bit confused, then said he'd stay only so long as he didn't cause any trouble for the only people he ever found worth living for. All his life, he had lived in this or that community. Here, he was a part of the community. Life would return to an empty farce if he were to lose that.

Nito nodded. "A point for murder, and one for suicide.

"Yajira, he spent some time with you. Did he do or say anything that could throw a little light on this mess, or did you have a feeling about him?"

"What do you mean about suicide?" Enrique asked.

"He said, at times, that he didn't think life was worth living before, and that he couldn't live if he brought anything bad to the people."

"Well, let's see if that would fit the way he died," Enrique suggested. "I think perhaps it doesn't, except in the condition he once said to me.

"He was talking about the ones he was hiding here from. He said that crossing people like that was no different than committing suicide, and that getting your throat cut was a natural death with them."

"Well ..." Nito said, with a grimace, "I still won't consider it natural death, if it was that.

"What we have is that he was found in the water by the dock. He died of drowning. There was a contusion on the right side of his head, just above the ear.

"The contusion could be because he fell against the boat when he slipped on the wet dock, which could mean an accident.

"It could have been struck by another person, he fell into the water, and drowned, which would mean murder.

"There was no one there we know about, so it could mean voodoo, considering that priest was here earlier."

"No," Yajira replied. "It was not the power, though it could be because he was given certain hallucinogens or a poison.

"Of course, those are voodoo, just not the psy power part. Voodoo or not, it would be murder."

"Yes, there is that. Was there any sign of heart failure, embolism, organ failure, Doc?"

"I imagine it could be an embolism. We don't have the facilities here to find it, if it was in the brain. His liver was not in bad condition, but was stressed, and he drank about two beers, earlier. He could have experienced a moment of vertigo while on the dock and fallen against the boat and into the water to drown, which would put it in the natural death category."

"So we haven't eliminated any explanation," Enrique said, with a sigh. "Yajira, can you tell us, definitely, it it was or was not voodoo?"

"It was not from a power, but could well be from a method, such as a poison.

"I would rule out hypnotism ... but maybe not. It could be because of a posthypnotic suggestion."

"Explain?"

"There was the amulet. That is an undeniable item. A connection.

"Perhaps not. There isn't any way any of them met with him here, and he has been away from them for more than a year, so ... it could be ...

"No. What could trigger it, after this time? He has been on that dock, with that boat, in that situation, many times. He was nowhere he could hear the voice or see the person. It would take a specific action, sight, or sound."

"But he would have seen and heard the person if they smacked him over the head there," Chapo pointed out.

Nito snorted, and said, "Yajira? How did he seem to you, and did your power tell you anything?"

"Other than that he was hiding from the devil, not much that I noted.

"I first met him when he came into the restaurant, the second day he was here, for almuerzo. I felt he was hiding from – or running from – something he felt to be dangerous and evil.

"I was coming in the door as he was just taking a seat at the table by the window...."

<u>*A Strange Conversation*</u>

"Hi! You're the medicine woman! Sam said you were, but I didn't think a medicine woman would be a pretty young ... Sorry! I always yap before I think!

"I'm Gordon Stevens. Gordy. From the United States."

"Yes. You are here to hide. There are dangerous people looking for you, and you fear they will kill you.

"You are an honest man, and are most uncomfortable, because you feel you will have to lie to us, and you do not believe it is right to lie, because it would mean you could never be friends with us, and you want to be friends, because you love the way we live.

"You do not have to lie. You are a good person, and one who likes to laugh and feel free with others."

"Sam said you would know everything about me with a look! He was right!

"I don't want to have to leave here. I only been here one night, and I love this place, and I love the people! No phony-ass bastards that ... sorry. Got to learn what not to say.

"I ain't never been anywhere like here! I ain't ... haven't ... I know how to talk, I'm just too lazy to ... anyhow, you aren't playing silly games. The ones I'm running from are the devil and her goons.

"I don't think they'll find me, here. I covered my tracks pretty good."

"No. You are carrying an amulet that tells someone where you are, generally, from a distance, and specifically, when close.

"Did you know that?"

"I *am*?! I didn't know! What is it?"

Yajira pointed to his chest, to a medallion he'd worn on a chain for years. He took it off and handed it to her.

"Can you block it, or something?"

"If you take it apart and put the crystals in places more than a few meters apart, it will inactivate. I feel it may be better to allow it to function, but not to be in a place where you are."

"So they will find it, but not me."

"Yes. It will be a temporary safety, in that it will allow you to know they are close, but they will not be where you are,"

"So that Liam creep would be the one. I always thought he was a creep. Voodoo high priest, or something.'

"Yes. Such things are used in the voodoo cults. It can make it seem a priest has a mental power that is greater than a simple talent that locates crystals set in certain patterns. There will be some fair confusion from distance, considering that the locators on thousands of cell phones are the same principal, just on different wave lengths."

"Who do you fear? Why?"

"My ex-wife, her family, and drug runners and dealers.

"I'll be honest with you. I don't think you'll care. She got me messed up with them. I can't live that way. I got my pride, and that makes me feel dirty in a way you can't wash it off.

"How come a medicine woman in the jungles of Panama knows about wave lengths and all that?"

Yajira laughed. "I'm a graduate of the University Oteima, in David. The times, as Dylan said, they are a'changin' all over the world."

"God, I love you people!"

"Hi, Jira! How are you this morning?"

"I am well. You seem in very good spirits!"

"Yeah. It's what you call a beautiful day, but they all are, here. Even when it's raining." He laughed. "Anything new? Were you looking for me?"

"Yes, and yes.

"Gordy, there are two people who came this morning on a boat from Chiriqui Grande. They are evil. They asked about you.

"Do you know Gladys and Liam, from Louisiana?"

"Gladys? Gladys Donelli? Dark hair, sort of good figure, wears too much lipstick, and that? Hard voice?

"Liam? I don't know who ... that big black who tries to look dangerous? Wears a lot of gold chains, and like that? Real slick, but phony? Always claims he has voodoo magic power?"

"Very apt descriptions. Liam has some slight power. He depends on his reputation to make people fear him. His face is a facade, as is his life. Not much is different about her, though her evil is deeper, and she has no power.

"Their intentions for you are not good. Either will kill you if they have the chance, but neither knows why, really.

"That is from the power. They try to present themselves as friends. They cannot lie to me. Liam senses I have power, and is afraid, but only that I will expose him for what he is.

"We told them you were not here, as Enrique suggested. He said we could say that, and be true about it, because we only say you left, and said maybe you will go toward Colombia. You did. We simply do not tell them you returned very soon."

"We still have nothing, as to the cause of death," Nito said, sourly. "It is likely, almost certain, he was murdered, but I don't know if it is a definition they'll accept outside of the comarca.

"I think I'll have to suggest we take a few hours to try to find what we can eliminate, in this case. Some things just don't fit."

"I will appoint you representative of the legal crap for the comarca," Silvio Smith Abrego, local chief, declared. "That makes it your responsibility. I'll get back to the cacao.

"What next? I don't know anything, except he was a good person in a bad situation."

"Maybe I can find some kind of clue at his place. To state it in a legal form, case is in recess until such time as we have something to report."

Nito went with Yajaira to the small house Gordy had used to see what clues he could find. He didn't expect much, but he'd learned, long ago, to not "expect" things. Too often, that led to disappointment, and little else.

They found a man there, just entering as they approached. He was trying to open the back door.

Nito was the police, such as they had. He was also appointed head of the investigation.

"Who are you, and what do you want here?" Nito asked.

"Uh, I just want to get some things for the dead man's wife. Family things, and like that.

"I'm Eddie Florenzi, from where he's from. New Orleans, you know. I work for his wife's, er, organization. Business. Like that."

"You didn't ask about it at the council building?" Yajaira asked, with a small smirk. "And why from the back door? The front door is open. We don't lock things here. We don't have many thieves or punk hoods running around, like in New Orleans."

"You might also explain how you knew which house, while you're at it," Nito added.

"Uh, a friend was here and came, so she told me. She's the one who said I should sort of, uh, collect some things for his wife."

"The Gladys Donelli woman? She never came anywhere near here. I don't think Liam did, either," Jira said. "They were both liars, like you. None of you were his friends, but that's because none of you *has* any friends." She winked at Nito. "The evidence stuff it at the council house. He gave it all to Silvio when those two first came here. In case any of you tried what you're trying.

"He said to not give it to anyone unless he was killed. Then we are to give it to a certain person who has connections in the states, and allow him to settle the matter. Leave the people out of it.

"Are you so stupid you will try to get the people involved in your sordid schemes?"

"It's all stuff we don't care about here. Gordy was a friend, and we want to know who to hold liable for his death. If it involves what Gordy called 'the material' it will be presented to the proper person, according to Gordy's wishes.

"I suggest you be off the comarca within the hour. If you killed him, you will be executed, if you're here."

"Hey! I didn't off anybody! He had a accident!

"Maybe Liam did something with that hoodoo stuff, but I didn't do nothing except come for his things for his wife!"

"There is nothing here for his wife. He was here to be away from her," Jira said. "I know you didn't kill him, and that you aren't sure he was killed, but that Liam and Gladys did it, if he was. I know you are here for the evidence of drug dealings in New Orleans, and of ... distribution? ... of the drugs and other things.

"I can kill you with a thought! Don't be more stupid than you already are by going for the knife in your sheath strapped to your leg! Your Liam has no real power! I *do*!"

"Oh, my God! Look, lady ... just let me go! I won't say anything! I swear! Just let me go! I won't never come back a hundred miles from this place! I swear!"

"Be off the comarca within the hour," Nito warned. "In one hour, I will declare you outlaw, and anyone who ever sees you on comarca land, at anytime, is instructed to chop you up with the handiest machete! Got it?"

Eddie broke into a run toward the dock.

"Papers? Evidence? You have the power to kill him with a thought?! Gee whiz!" Nito said, laughing.

Yajiara laughed. "Well, it's okay to lie to a liar, and he believes I have the power. I could sense he was looking for some papers of for a ... memory stick? Disc? CD? All of them? Any of them?"

Nito nodded. "Let's see if we can eliminate the

voodoo bit, at least. Maybe we can, by using it, ourselves!"

They went around front and in the open door. Inside was Spartan, but clean. There was a small table with a laptop computer on it. There was a tray of CDs, and a little box with several memory sticks in it.

"Our evidence will be there," Nito said, pointing. "I want to know how he died, and if it really was suicide.

"I tend to doubt it."

"As do I. Perhaps he left a note, if it was. It would be on the screen at boot-up."

There was a large paper sack on the kitchen table. It was from the almacen near the dock. Nito looked inside.

"A dozen eggs. A liter of milk. Corn flakes. Rice. Flour. Sugar. Onions. Soap, both for the lavadora and the shower. A dish pad.

"Suicide is out, at least. Nobody with even a slight tendency for suicide would buy stuff for the next couple of weeks the day they committed suicide."

Jira nodded. "Suicide is out. I think accident is also out. Murder is in, even if it was by voodoo, or whatever. I think natural causes are unlikely.

"By what is called 'the preponderance of the evidence' outside, we have established murder."

"Now to establish why, though I think I know.

Those people are incredibly stupid. If therte was one thing they could have counted on, it was that Gordy wouldn't ever use what he had against them if they would just leave him alone."

"They lead their empty lives in constant fear that others will somehow expose them for what they are."

Nito sighed, sadly, and nodded grimly. "So let's make their worst fears come true, like in the song."

"Song?"

"Pink Floyd. *Mother*. 'Mama's gonna make all of your nightmares come true...' Only it ain't Mama who's going to do it."

"I haven't listened to Pink Floyd for years."

Nito gave her the bird. "What was that about the stuff Gordy left at the council for if he was murdered? Why didn't I know about it?"

"Because I made it up. It's the kind of thing from the TV detective shows from the states. What they call 'blackmail insurance' papers. It was accepted as truth by him. He is a liar, so I will lie to him. It as much as terrifies him that it could be true. He feels he has to tell ... someone he considers his boss. Hi will be held responsible for msome reason I can't understand, and I have no idea what it is he will be responsible for.

"He is afraid they will kill him. His entire life is fear.

"Welcome to life in the fast lane in the states."

"The investigation has led us to a conclusion of murder by person or persons unknown. Due to other information gathered, the investigation will continue," Nito reported. "We will report what we find as quickly as practical.

"This is due to the fact Gordy was a friend of the comarca. His death must not be for nothing."

Everyone nodded their agreement with that.

"Nito, there are two more of those greedy cheap thugs just coming in at the dock," Silvio said. "Luis called me from Chiriqui Grande and said they were coming. He checked their ID for the police. They are from Louisiana, and are in the trucking business. One of them is staying in Chiriqui Grande, a woman. She complains all the time, and is going to Bocas, where there are hotels she might just barely be able to tolerate."

"Name wouldn't be Gordon, would it?" Yajaira asked.

"Part. It's Glenda Roberts-Feratti. Ex-wife of Gordon Roberts. She was going to come to the comarca with another woman by the name of Gladys Something-or-other, who is persona non grata on the comarca for some trivial no-meaning misunderstanding."

"Liam with them?"

"No. Maybe she's meeting him in Bocas. He

hasn't left Panama."

"Well, let's get into the computer crap. Maybe we can tell them all about what they're after."

"It's your problem. I say we go to the hotel and tell them to get their sorry asses off the comarca," Silvio replied, drily. "I'm just the damned chief, so nobody will listen to me, anyhow."

Nito et al gave him the bird.

Nito booted up Gordy's old laptop. Gordy had never said he had any information there about the bunch in Louisiana, but he wouldn't. That would put the people in danger, and he would not do that. Gordon had been a very good person, deep down, who was in a very hard – if not impossible – situation.

That he had made up some kind of insurance information against he ex-wife's goon squad, he didn't doubt. He wouldn't want anyone on the comarca to know.

That the Eddie character was here meant she thought that was true left no doubt.

Everything seemed dull and normal on the computer. Three hours of searching everything there l;ed to that conclusion.

That meant the CDs or memory sticks.

One stick, 4 GIGs, was pictures with numbers. They were pictures of everything from flowers to birds to people to towns and cities, to ocean scenes, to ship ports and airports to carports.

That some of those pictures were important was a given, but which ones, and why? The numbers were the ... but not unless he had some kind of list that attached the pictures to specific things.

Nito thought for awhile, shrugged, and put in the next stick, It was a copy of three CDs he had already read.

He put in another. It was a document file with an extension that there was no program in place to open. The notation asked if he wished to search the internet for a program that would read it.

He took the USB modem to find it was one that worked through the iPhone or Claro system, and there was no saldo.

He took a break, went to the cantine for a Claro tarjeta, had a beer, and went back to buy a week of internet connection, then back to search for a program that would open the file.

No compatible program found. Shit!

Did that mean Gordy had made his own program? Did he know enough about computers to do that?

Nito remembered the old Atari his father had. It had a "basic" system that allowed anyone to design a program. It didn't take a lot of knowledge or skill. Gordy would have been about ten years old when that was the best computer you could get.

He probably had used an old Tandy or Atari and had made his own program. Nito went to the list and said to translate into ASCII.

A bunch of meaningless symbols.

Was Doug still alive – no. He died last year. He could have fixed that problem in ten minutes.

He sighed, put the stick aside, and took the next. It was photocopies of titles, insurance policies, trucking schedules, and other things to do with his trucking business.

Why did he keep them"

DUH! Because they connected some things! Now to find the things they connected!

Like a stick he couldn't read and the numbers on photos, probably.

He put the last three sticks into the USB ports and spent 4 hours going through them. Nothing.

Except? Were the date on the correspondence files important? Were *they* the necessary connection points to everything else?

It would wait until morning. It was after eight, he was tired and hungry, and he wanted to be with his wife and kids.

There was a hbub in the little car as he passed on his way to his house. He stepped in, and saw two strangers. Danelo said they came in earlier, and were making asses of themselves. They thought they could give orders.

He explained that it was a mite late to have to be off the comarca within the hour or be declared outlaw, which would result in their executions. Perhaps they should consider acting like human beings instead of pigs to avoid that possiibility.

"Who the fuck is that asshole?" the big one asked Juian, the bartender.

"Nito? He's acting chief. We have to do what he says, so hope he doesn't say to chop you up with our machetes."

"You got a machete, I got a Glock!"

"You got a Glock, and we got fifty machetes. Let Nito find out you have a gun on the comarca and you're cut fish bait in two minutes!" He winked at Nito, who was, unbeknownst to the hood, right behind him. "You got fifty rounds in your Glock?"

He looked like he'd been slapped in the face with a rotten fish. He shut up and sat down.

"Juan, one more instance, you call me. We see how these cruds are in the water on a moonless night, having to get out of comarca area in an hour, or be tried as thugs."

"We got a law about that?" Juan asked, grinning.

"I'm acting chief. I'll make one up."

Juan laughed. "Okay. See you in the morning. Find anything in those computer things?"

"Oh, yeah! Maybe."

They waved. Nito went home.

Nito booted the computer. He grinned at the symbol in the lower left corner of the screen. The computer had been used since he left last night.

He expected that, thus the symbol.

Jira came in to hand him a large mug of strong coffee. "I saw you were here late last night, so knew you'd be here this morning.

"I heard about the bar. I went in after you left. Those two were scared half out of their skulls. They were bluffing, and Juan saying they could be chopped up if they brought guns onto the comarca terrifies them. I think that was a little detail Glennie-wenda left out when she gave them their orders. We now have two oversized wharf rats in a place where wharf rats are not feared, they're eliminated.

"Gonzo and Smitty.

"Find anything?"

"Yes, but I can't read it. Do you know anything about programming computers?"

"A little. A *very* little."

"I have a stick that I can't read. The net doesn't have a compatible program to read it."

"Read it in basic ASCII."

"No go."

"Hmm. There will be a program, somewhere.

"I read all of it. I didn't find one."

"Well, what did you find?"

"A lot of pictures. Records. Business. Normal stuff."

"You read all the CDs and the sticks? I think you...!"

"The camera! Was there a camera in his place?"

"Yes. It's in the cabinet with his personal stuff. Why?"

"Something my Pop did, one time. He wanted to hide some info, but knew they would check everything in the place that had to do with the comp." He went to the cabinet and took the camera to the table, turned it on, and clicked on the menu. It said, "Twenty four pictures" and brought the last one taken to screen. He went back through all of them, but they were just pictures of the people and the area.

He took the chip out and inserted it into the laptop slot. He clicked on *Open the device to view contents* and clicked on *mprgs* file.

AUTORUN Windows Installer came onscreen.

"*Yes*!" he and Jira cried at the same time.

"The camera has a standard eight GIG memory card," Nito explained. "No one thinks of looking in a camera memory for a program!?

"You did.

"Nito! Someone evil is coming!"

"Delay them two minutes. Outside!"

Jira ran to open the door. The thug called Gonzo was just outside. She greeted him and asked what he was looking for at the council house. He needed permission to go inside. He was not of the people.

"I just wanna check on the stuff from Robert's place for his old lady."

"Robert who? Why would we have any stuff from him?"

"No, Gordon Roberts. The guy who had a accident the other day. His wife wants to know if he had anything worth getting."

"Oh. All his things will be given to the police in David. She can check it there, if she wants. I think there was an old computer, and a camera, but not a very expensive one. The freight to the states is more than they're worth."

"She wants the business records. She has to run it, now."

"Business?"

"He had this here trucking company. She gets it."

"Well, Nito is inside, and he would know about that kind of thing. You can go in. I give permission."

"You an official?"

"Official? Official what?"

"That you can give permission. That kind of official."

"No. I am Ngobe. I can give permission. It is as much my council house as it is anyone's.

"I can't – and don't – give permission for you to take anything out."

"Yeah. Okay. Thanks."

She waved and went on toward the dock. Gonzo looked confused, shrugged, started to say something, shrugged again, and went inside, where Nito was laying back in a chair, drinking his coffee.

"Uh, you the guy in charge here?" Gonzo asked.

"As much as anyone, I guess. Can I help you with something?"

"I gotta see the, uh, the papers from Roberts' stuff. For the widow, you know. They sent me to get it. She has to run the trucking company and that kind of crap. Has to have the records to see who to send what to."

"Widow? He was divorced. She has no recourse to his things not specifically relegated to her in written form – Whatever that means. We give it all to the police in David, you get anything from there. I just boxed it up and sent it to them.

"They want us to officially declare what he died from, and we can't get it, definitely, so I guess they'll hold it until we find out how he died."

"What do you mean? He had a accident!"

"Not likely. Medical examiner said he was hit over the head, so it wasn't any accident."

"He fell into the water and hit his head on a boat or, uh, something like that!"

"The ME said there was no hair or blood or anything on the boat, or anywhere else. Didn't happen that way."

"You check that kind of stuff, here in the jun ... uh, medical examiner? You have a medical examiner here?"

"Sure! We aren't a bunch of savages living a hundred years ago!"

"Uh, well, I mean ... all I need is some business papers, or from the computer crap, or like that."

"You have to get it in David when they release it. I looked at all of it. Nothing worth the trouble, and the only things about the business was from when he sold it, so his ex-wife wouldn't need it, even if she does get anything because he's dead.

"He took a lot of pictures. I had to look at all of them, for some reason. Said I'd know if I found anything, but I didn't find anything,except stuff like everybody takes."

"Did you look at, like, the other stuff in the computer?"

"Every little thing. Took me more than nine

hours. For nothing. Maybe the stuff he sent the night before he died means something, but he sent it and erased it."

"Erased it? Then how do you know he sent anything?"

"Upload to some gov address. Maybe taxes or something."

"Gov address? What's that?"

"Got me! It was to, let me think, um, o-c-c-m-s dot gov – or that kind of thing. I can look it up, I guess, The computer's still online. I was just having a coffee break."

Nito went to the computer. He was having a hard time not laughing in the hood's face, the way he was sweating and stammering. He was pasty white and *very* sick looking. Nito remembered the old Country song. "like a dyin' calf in a hailstorm" kind of thing.

"Hmm. o-c-c ... here it is. Organized crime commission senate. Must have known something about a politician. Maybe that was why he was hiding here. Maybe we can find out ... who cares? It doesn't have anything to do with us. I do think that makes the evidence say he was murdered by person or persons unknown. Never find anything about politicians or drug cartels. Not worth investigating – which we wouldn't, anyhow, except he was a friend."

Gonzo as much as ran toward the cantina,

where the only public telephone could be found.

He didn't buy a throwaway when he came? Incompetent moron!

Nito remembered a comment on FB. "Impotent maroon!" He giggled.

Then he went back to read that stick with the special program.

<u>*Hot Water. Very Hot Water*</u>

The first thing that came up was a list that was just numbers in sets. The same numbers on those photos.

That was obvious enough.

Date in photo

He brought a photo to screen. There was no date.

Wait! Date *in* photo!

He right-clicked on the photo.

13:21 10/14/11. It was a picture of a boat at a dock. The Horizon Star.

Was it important? Was it just a picture?

Obviously, the boat was the subject, but why? A drug runner?

Not big enough, and unlikely. It was a fishing boat. A little fancy, but a fishing boat.

He went back to the card. The numbers list was there, labeled *nmb-pic*.

He went back to the photo, and put it on split screen. It was picture #1 on the card.

#1: transfer boat, NO, GDY dock

What the hell was GDY dock? This was, he supposed, a boat used to transfer drugs from a larger boat somewhere in the closer area.

It was only a claim. A picture of a boat at a dock was evidence that a boat, that one, was at a dock at a specific time. Big deal!

That wasn't fair. It would be explained later.

He looked further along the list, where there were some notes, at the end of the list:

ADSN W – William Anderson

Anld B – Arnold Bettancourt

G FKN – Gino Franketti

KL SC – Karl Schmidt

Followed by nine more names.

D WRH – Doniletti warehouse, CDY dock

EC 7th – electronic consultant

GRY – Grady warehouse [dock-Bayou Court - LeGrange Road]

MTN – Milton warehouse [dock-Baton Rouge]

So. The picture was a runner boat at the Grady dock warehouse.

There were four more places, a break, and three residences, followed by two restaurants and the race track. There was a *tx-N671/Bartlet* at the end of that page.

There were several pictures of a taxi with people getting in or out. It was taxi N-671.

Now to list the pictures and the information. It was going to take hours to go through all of them.

Was this going to expose a big drug distribution ring?

There were several pictures of people loading

or unloading a truck – trucks – with numbers. Most were MT-1, MT-2, and MT-3.

The list. *MT – my truck [1-2-3-4]*

There was a location after each picture, listing the place. The date and time was on, rather, *in*, the picture.

Some of the things being loaded or unloaded were possibly drugs, but some were as definitely not.

Well, if all this crap had to be listed and identified, might as well get at it!

It was after 2:00AM. Nito had been at it for 16 hours. He had it all listed, in chronological order. Everyone was identified. All locations were pinpointed on a map he'd downloaded from MapQuest. A 1.13 GIG file was built. There were four copies, plus the original, which was included on the memory sticks.

Nito was tired – exhausted – hungry, and in a foul mood. There was no one on the street. Everything, including the cantina, was closed.

That was why he noticed a slight movement ahead. A shadow from a streetlight behind someone ahead.

Damn! He didn't have his pistol!

Well, they probably wouldn't dare use one. They were warned that even having one here could result in them being "executed" with dull machetes.

He was suddenly very glad his father, the famous Clint Faraday, has taught him some Taekwon-do and some plain-out old street fighting maneuvers from the states! He was also glad he had such good peripheral vision. Not as good as Clint's, but far more than most!

He knew a trick or two!

He dropped the file he was carrying, and bent down to pick it up. He also picked up a smooth rock, the size of an orange.

He passed a little out from the corner where he'd noticed the shadow. A form dodged out behind him and reached for him.

He spun, slapped the rock just over the left ear of the thug. It wasn't, as he expected, Gonzo. This must be the one they called "Smitty."

He sighed, patted down the thug's unconscious body, took the .32 automatic from the holster just under his crotch, and the knife from the sheath in the middle of his lower back, along the spine, just at the belt line.

He cupped his hand and carried a little of the rainwater at the gutter to throw in the hood's face.

"Smitty" sat up, suddenly, and reached for his back.

"I have it, and the pistol. I'm trained in methods to kill you with a flick of the wrist. The course also taught how to instill pain that you couldn't possible imagine, so don't be too stupid. I'm tired and in a bad move.

"All you needed to do was to ask for what you want. I would tell you, or would say to fuck off.

"So! What do you want?"

"Geez! I just was going to ask about some papers, or like that!"

"For that, you hide and come from behind? Really?

"I warned you not to be too stupid. You might irritate me."

"I wasn't going to hurt you! Just knock you out and get the stuff."

"I'm not carrying anything that I would keep from you, if you asked. Everything was already sent to the police in David and Panama City."

"Geez! I tried to tell them you were too sharp to carry anything! I told them! They made me do it!"

"I don't doubt that. There wasn't anything about you or Gonzo in the files. A couple of pictures where you were off to the side, but nothing that could cause you any problems.

"I have a question for you. It was mostly drugs, but some of it wasn't. I suppose it was jewels or art or gold or whatever. There were some things where ... I couldn't see what was going on."

"Geez! You got all that, and you just tell me? I don't believe you! You aren't real!

"I can't figure why ... I mean, are you for real?"

"I found it. I don't have it, anymore. The police in David have it, or will, when they get the correspondence in the morning. I imagine they'll get it to the embassy in Panama City in five minutes, after they see what it is.

"That will give you time to get out. If you try to protect anyone not right here, you'll stay that one minute too long, and end up in the pen for the rest of your life, or worse.

"For this kind of stuff, all they will want you for is witnesses. After the trials, they won't bother about you.

"Be somewhere they can't find you and can't get you to the states without a lot more BS than it's worth. You can get to Venezuela, easy. They aren't going to get into that kind of tangle.

"Warn the lovely lady and her friends, you won't get to Venezuela. Capich?"

"Yeah. I said you were too sharp for them, but they don't never listen to us peons.

"You're okay. You give a guy a break.

"What do you mean about ... that stuff? You don't grab?"

"People like some man called Garibaldi. What was he into? Adolf Myers? Donaldo Gutierez? What were they even in the records for?"

"Them? They were illegal. Sort of what you call persona none gracias in the states because of some 'indiscretions,' like."

"Oh. *They* were what was smuggled."

"Yeah. Feds get all upset because they come and go, and they can't find out how."

"Well, it's almost three. I think you should be gone before daylight. Take Gonzo with you, if that would be cool."

"You, I like, You could be a pal.

"I know it's crazy to ask, but could I have the piece back? You can keep the bullets. I won't try anything. I swear. I might need it if they sent some people to, sort of, talk to me, if you know what I'm saying.

"How do you ... how can I get out of here? They'll come after me in a blink!"

"You and Gonzo. Nobody else. Get the boat and go east. Stay more than two hundred feet offshore. You can get to the islands before the canal. Trade the boat for whatever, and get to Venezuela.

"People start work as soon as it's light enough. You have about an hour and a half, so you can be too far for them to get to you."

"Yeah! That's right! They have to have the boat to get anywhere, and it'll be gone! It'll take them at least three hours to get someone here!"

"Move! You don't have any time to waste!

"Here." He gave him the pistol and knife. "Don't let anyone know you have this, on the comarca. That they'll chop you into fish bait is no joke, and it's no bluff.

"Do they have anyone watching the boat?"

"Yeah! Gonzo!"

Nito laughed. Smitty grinned. "I think I ... I wish I could stay. You're a friend, and I don't have any others."

"Be a friend, and you have a friend. Go!"

Smitty bolted toward the dock.

Nito went home to his wife and family.

Nito's son, Guilermo, came to wake him and say Silvio was in the kitchen and wanted to talk with him. [The people talk *with* each other, not *to* each other.] "Something about cheap thugs, and like that, and he wants to know what he's supposed to do with the printout in English, and the memory stick."

"Umm. Okay. I'll be right in."

"You look like you should be getting into bed, not getting out."

"Not nearly as much as I *feel* like that!" He tousled Mo's hair and got up. Mo went back into the kitchen.

Nito splashed cool water on his face, looked in the mirror, grimaced, and went into the kitchen. He poured a large mug of coffee, and sat across the table from Silvio.

"Nito, what in hell is going on with that bunch of silly clowns? Why did the two hoods get in their cigarette boat and take off toward the canal? What is this crap you left in the council house for me? Why are those two assholes, that woman who's harder than steel and the man who she treats like he treats everyone else running around, saying we have to get them to Chiriqui Grande, *right now!*, or there will be big problems for all of us....

"In other words, why do things always go into deep shit when I leave you in charge of anything?"

"It keeps me from getting bored.

"They're big-time criminals in the states, and Gordy left the proof. He didn't ever want it to be needed, and he tried to keep us out of it. If they hadn't killed him, none of the rest would have happened, and we'd never know what he was hiding from here.

"Is the woman here his ex-wife? Who is the man?"

"Yes. She presented papers saying she was Mary Ann Matthews, but Ernesto, in Chiriqui Grande checker her passport. It wasn't the same as the papers she showed us.

"Are those people as stupid as they seem? Why did she show us any papers, at all, if she didn't want us to know? She as much as demanded that we see the papers. We don't give a shit."

"She didn't want us to connect her with Gordy – so she tried to make it seem she was just a tourist."

"Why else would she be here to ask all the questions about him? As I said, are they really that stupid?"

"They watch too much TV.

"Did you send the stuff I left to David?"

"Yes. It took more than five minutes to send the memory stick. That's a *lot* of data!"

"It took me sixteen hours to type it all up and correlate it. It will result in another big drug bust, along with a lot of other things, that will cause maybe a two minute pause in the international crime syndicate business.

"I did it for Gordy. He was a good person."

"Yes. I liked Gordy.

"I do *not* like his ex-wife. I have never wanted to hit a woman before, but I would, with great glee, smack her capped teeth down her throat for her.

"She yells at me that I will arrange for her to get to Chiriqui Grande, in less than an hour, or I will regret it! Do I know who she *is*?!

"I said she was Mrs. Gordon Roberts, who had presented false papers upon coming here, and that I could put her in a cell for the next ninety days for that, and that there are a lot more charges I can cite, and does she have her toothbrush and all that with her?

"She almost fainted. The turkey with her kept saying, 'See here! See here!' I said 'See what? That she's an obnoxious criminal?' and he looked like *he* would faint!"

Nito laughed. "Sort of typical of the type."

"She said she would have a voodoo priest come and curse the comarca, and, particularly, me!

"Juan told me all about those other characters, so I said, if she meant that Liam clown, Yajira, our own voodoo priestess, had already shown him up as a trickster with no real power – and she *does* have power!

"Her mouthy friend said she had been warned about that, and it wasn't very wise to make such a claim.

"She could have fried him with a look!

"Then they sort of begged me to get them away. They would make it worth my trouble. They would give me fifty thousand dollars if they could be gone before anyone came for them!

"I said I had nothing I could spend any fifty dollars, much less fifty thousand, on here.

"They are trying to get someone to take them in a boat, but they don't speak Spanish, much less Ngobere. Her doggie man tries to talk in French, and we pretend nobody here speaks that, either.

"Nito, what are we going to do with you? Every time some crooked gringo come to Panama, they come here, and you get all involved in some kind of mess we don't even understand!"

Someone was calling for Silvio from the water. They went onto the porch, and Omar, a fisherman, said that Juan called for a helicopter to take the crazy gringos away. They would pay for it.

"He said to tell you he called the police in David to tell them the helicopter was going there. Was that alright?"

"Yes. It will solve most of our problems, I suppose," Silvio replied. "Thanks, Omar."

Omar waved and went on to collect conch for the market in Chiriqui Grande.

"Well, that should leave none of them in Cusapin," Silvio said. "Please wait at least a week before you bring anymore of the type here. We need the rest!"

"Speaking of rest, I'm going back to bed."

Silvio laughed. "Are you suggesting something?"

"No. I'm too tired. Talk to me after I get another six hours of sleep."

They gave each other the bird.

Silvio headed up the beach toward Cusapin. Nito went back to bed.

"It's been a bit of fun in town," Yajira said. "Some clown from the CIA was with another one from the FBI. They said they were here to take you to the United States to testify in the Feratti Syndicate investigation.

"They didn't know who you were. Juan left that off of the stuff he gave them. He just said you were a Ngobe.

"They started with the usual demands and

orders. Solvio came in, and they said they would bring the police from Panama City to arrest you, if you didn't come with them, and right *now*!

"I was standing there like a stump, and said they didn't know who you were, but they would arrest you?

"The Johnson character, the FBI idiot, said they wouyld find that out in two minutes.

"Silvio said less than that. You were Clinton Fadaday Abrego, son of the famous Clinton Faraday, and they could talk directly to you with their threats. Just walk about a kilometer up the beach, and here you'd be!"

"They coming?"

"No. They asked me, very politely, if I would please request that you come to Cusapin for a friendly chat and maybe a lunch in the restaurant *they* would pay for. It is a matter of great urgency,. and they are sure you will want to hear of the events that led them to come here."

"So you came? I'm disappointed!" He grinned. She smirked.

"I said I had to meet with some paying clients, and would come either later today or maybe tomorrow. Or next day. They could just walk up the beach and talk to you here. They didn't need me.

"They gave me a hundred dollars."

"Well! How cheap! It took you all of a quarter

hour, and will take another quarter to get back! A whole half hour of your time for only a hundred bucks?! How cheap!"

They laughed. "You going?" she asked.

"Yeah. I'll walk you back, to be sure you're safe."

"Well, I might be raped, and that wouldn't happen if you were there.

"Do you think you could wait an hour, then go?"

They called that they were going to Cusapin. Mo said he wanted to go, to see how Dad handled the arrogant gringo morons. They headed up the beach, laughing and playing jokes.

"Why don't they just come to the house and talk to you?" Mo asked.

"They tried that with Dad. Several times. It doesn't go so well for them to do that."

"Besides, they would rather pay me to go, so they don't have to walk all that way for nothing," Jira said.

They came into Cusapin, to find Johnson and Smith [Yeah. Right!] waiting in the cantina. Nito pulled up a chair for Jira, and he and Mo sat in the other chairs. Johnson and Smith introduced themselves. Clint introduced Mo.

"You want a kid to hear this stuff?" Smith said, sarcastically.

"Smith!" Johnson warned.

"Shit! I say we take this one to the chopper and stop wasting time!" Smith spat.

"Another one of those doofuses?" Mo asked.

"Yeah. They do get boring, don't they?" Jira answered. "I'll have the chuleta with yuca and lentajas. Mo?"

"Pollo patio. Rice with parotos. Fried banana with honey. Guanabana chicha."

"Corvina. Papas pure'. Guanabana chicha, and coffee," Nito ordered. The girl at the counter nodded and turned in the order.

"Okay. What?" Nito asked.

"You decoded that crap in the Roberts case?" Smith asked.

"Some of it. Why?"

"We need you to testify how you did it, and all that," Johnson said. "We have to present you for sworn testimony, and you have to explain for the court what you did and how you did it."

"No I don't. That's all in the sworn and certified affidavit that we sent with the evidence."

"See here! We don't have time for this! You have to be there for questioning by the defense! Just pack your things and come along, and there won't be any problems!"

"Fuck you! It's all handled in affidavit, and there is no reason to question anything other than how I found the evidence, and how I handled it. That's handled.

"You've had your little vacation. Now go back where you came from and don't bother anyone on the comarca again."

"As soon as I found out who we were dealing with, I told Smith we were wasting our time. It can only lead to problems for us." Johnson said. "I will ask you to come. It's paid for."

"I have several million dollars in the bank from my father. I'm not about to go to the states.

"You might ask yourselves what you're doing here. This is all handled through international agreements. *Why* were you sent?"

"It's our job! I'm not about to leave here without you!" Smith ranted.

"Smith! Shut up!" Johnson snapped. "We have no authority here!"

"We have an agreement with Panama about extradition!"

"You don't have one with the comarca," Jira said. "We operate under comarca laws, not Panamanian law."

"I know that. It's why I already said we should just forget the routine," Johnson said. "Mr. Faraday, what do you mean? I admit to some suspicion about why we were sent."

"The courts know, full well, the arrangements with Panama and the comarca. My father pounded that into you, repeatedly and forcefully, a long time ago.

"I suggest you very carefully check out any judge that would allow this tactic, much less become part of it."

"So somebody paid off a judge. Happens all the time, even in Panama."

"It don't happen on the comarca." Mo said.

"'Doesn't' happen. Find out which coin that judge was paid in," Jira said. "Flan! You have flan! I'll take some!"

"Me, too!" Mo cried.

Joyhnson looked thoughtful. Smith looked like his head would boil.

"They can throw out the testimony if you can't be questioned! You *will* go back with us!" Smith cried.

"No, they can't," Smith replied, very silkily. "I begin to wonder why you are so adamant about a lost cause. I wonder greatly. You have no personal stake in it!

"*Do* you?"

"What? I just ... we came all the way out here, and I won't ... that is, we have a job to do, and I intend to do it!"

"You exceed the parameters of your job description," Jira said, smugly. "Did they tell you I know a lie, or subterfuge, or false face? It's my talent, and I'm never wrong?

"Agent Johnson, this person is not who he pretends to be. How carefully did you investigate *him*?"

"Apparently, not carefully enough. I guaran-damned-tee you that little oversight will be dealt with.

"You look a lot like the pictures of Mathilde."

"She was my mother. I have her talent."

Johnson nodded. "Well, we will pay for the meal and head back to Panama City. Sorry to have bothered you."

He stood. Smith was sweating.

"My God! They have my wife and daughter! I *had* to do it!"

"Arnie? What's going on!?" Johnson cried.

"Oh, God! They'll kill them! Oh, God!"

"I'll talk to you, now!" Nito promised. "Smith, can we stall them? For a few hours?"

"Oh, God!"

"You have a way to contact them?" Nito asked.

"Yes ... I think so. I'm to call a number when we have you in Panama City. They said all we have to do is get you there, and they'll handle it from that point."

"I don't see what it would accomplish. If they get me off the comarca, they can extradite me, for cause.

"Did you have any physical contact with any of them?"

"Just some weird character they call Ahmed. He was just delivering a message, though. He isn't one of them."

Nito stopped to recall ... and smirked. "No, he wasn't. Let's go to Panama City – with a written agreement that I will be free to come and go as I please, and that I am not subject to extradition.

"Smith, we can do something that will make it easy for *you* to testify! It'll rid the world of another bunch of scum!"

Smith looked terrified, but nodded.

"So! Let's get this play on the stage!" Nito said.

"Does this mean I have to go back home and tell Mom you won't be there for supper – again?" Mo asked, with a grin.

"Yup! I should be back by this time ... I have to get some things from the house. It'll take about an hour to go there, get it, and come back."

"We have the chopper. Five minutes each way," Johnson said.

"Then I can eat the flan before we go."

The chopper landed at just before six o'clock at the Albrook airport. Smith went inside and made a phone call. Nito and Johnson waited in the com shed.

"Okay. What now?" Johnson asked.

"I have to see who's watching."

They stood around, then Smith came back and said he reported they were there. They were to wait for the car to take them to HQ. Quietly, he said he called, and was told a car would be sent. It wouldn't be the FBI car.

Nito saw a swarthy man who was cleaning a nearby chopper go into the booth to make a call.

"They don't give them throwaways?" Nito asked. "How strange!"

"They said I wasn't to use mine. It was too easy to trace," Smith replied.

"You two go out front while he's in the booth and can't see you."

They headed out. Nito went behind a stack of boxes to wait. The man came back, looked around, and headed for the front. A car came, about three minutes later, and they got in. There were people around, and the watcher couldn't see how many got in the car.

The car left. The watcher went to an older Honda and got in. Nito grabbed a cab, and said to follow, and don't be seen doing it. He showed the cabbie a fifty dollar bill, which got a nod. They followed the car at a distance, until it turned off the main road onto a suburban street. They went past the street, then turned around and headed back to it.

It was houses with driveways, which made it upper middle class. The car was parked in the carport of a house on the fourth block in.

Nito paid the cabbie, and said he never saw him before, that he took a woman called Maria to a house a block back. The cab left, after asking what it was about.

A cheap gigolo meeting with his wife. If he showed up dead, it would be a bad idea to ever mention being in the area.

The cabbie left. Suddenly and quickly.

Nito called Smith and said there was a good chance he had found where they were keeping his wife and daughter. He gave the address, and said to get there in ten minutes or less.

He waited. Six minutes later, the car came down the block and stopped beside him. He was waiting on the sidewalk.

"What do we do?" Smith asked, shaking.

"You stay in th car. Johnson, you come with

me. You go around back. I'll go to the front door when you're there. Anybody comes out of that house, you handcuff them around a tree or something. Silently."

Johnson nodded, and took a Glock from a hidden holster.

Nito took his own .32 from the holster in back, put it in his pocket with his hand on it, waited two minutes, and went to the door to call, "Buenas!" as was the custom.

The swarthy man answered the door, a look of shock on his face when he saw Nito standing there.

"Ah! Ahmed, wasn't it? I saw you in Cusapin, just a couple of days ago!

"I'm afraid you're in a lot more trouble than you can ever get out of. We frown on kidnapping and all that klind of thing, here in Panama.

"Well? Aren't you going to invite me in?"

Ahmed tried to slam the door. Nito shoved it open, and he ran toward the back of the house. Another man stepped into the hall, and turned to follow Ahmed. A woman's voice asked what the hell was going on. She stepped into the hall, looked at the retreating backs of Ahmed and his follower, then at Nito.

"Hi! Sort of nervous types, eh what?"

She went back into the room and slammed the door. There was the sound of a little girl, crying.

Nito's shoulder hit the door, splintering the catch. It probably wasn't locked, but he must move fast. He drew the pistol and waved it at the woman, who was looking for something in a drawer.

"Come up with a gun, you're headed for the morgue!"

She slowly took her hand out of the drawer and raised it.

There was a woman on the bed. Unconscious or drugged. A girl, about 4 years old, was in a chair, crying.

"It's okay, Honey. It's all over, now. Your father will be here in a minute.

"You, m'dear [to the woman] will have a long-term address, soon, where we can reach you. I'm afraid it won't be too comfortable, but that's the way it goes."

Smith burst into the room and ran to hug the little girl. The woman on the bed groaned and tried to sit up – which relieved Nito, immensely.

"Okay. Let's wrap this up. I want to get back to my family."

"I'll carry you on my back, if necessary," Smith said, solemnly.

Johnson came into the room. Ahmed and the other man were handcuffed together in the hall.

"We have a lot of forms to fill out first," he pointed out.

"No. You do!" Nito replied, happily. "I have my whole part of it here." He took out the little camera/recorder and unclipped it from his pocket. "Ain't modern technology a hoot?"

"Smith called and told me about the whole thing," Nito reported. "The two here were given the choice of spending twenty years for kidnaping a minor or going to the states to testify, then be put on a WP program.

"They might survive a year.

"After the conviction of seventeen major international drug and other smugglers, with the added charges of bringing in illegal declared criminals for cash, ex-wife and two friends were informed that, after they served their two hundred seventy years, they would be extradited to Panama to face murder charges.

"All-in-all, not so bad!"

"That's nice. Are we going fishing like you promised?" Mo asked.

C. D. Moulton's works are available on most major outlets as printed or e-books. CD writes the CD Grimes, PI, mysteries, the Det. Lt. Nick Storie mysteries, the Clint Faraday mysteries, the Flight of the Maita science fiction series, books on orchid culture and many others of many types. Mystery, adventure, intrigue, science fiction, humor, fantasy, paranormal, mild erotica, and factual.